W9-BPM-846

j398.24
PER

The Lion and the Mouse

HOMEWOOD PUBLIC LIBRARY

RETOLD AND ILLUSTRATED BY GRAHAM PERCY

OCT - - 2009

For Robert

Distributed in the United States of America by
The Child's World®
1980 Lookout Drive • Mankato, MN 56003-1705
800-599-READ • www.childsworld.com

ACKNOWLEDGMENTS
The Child's World®: Mary Berendes, Publishing Director
The Design Lab: Kathleen Petelinsek, Art Direction and Design;
Anna Petelinsek, Page Production

COPYRIGHT
Copyright © 2010 by The Peterson Publishing Company. All rights reserved.
No part of this book may be reproduced or utilized in any form
or by any means without written permission from the publisher.

LIBRARY OF CONGRESS CATALOGING-IN-PUBLICATION DATA
Percy, Graham.
 The lion and the mouse / retold and illustrated by Graham Percy.
   p. cm. — (Aesop's fables)
 Summary: A retelling of the well-known fable in which a little mouse saves
the life of the King of Beasts.
 ISBN 978-1-60253-203-8 (lib. bound : alk. paper)
 [1. Fables. 2. Folklore.] I. Aesop. II. Title.
 PZ8.2.P435Li 2009
 398.2—dc22
 [E]   2009001589

A good deed should be returned.

One day, a tiny mouse was rushing through the forest. She carried an ear of wheat. It was going to be a nice meal for her children.

The mouse hurried to get home, for her children were all alone. But she was also very tired. Just then, she came to a soft, brown tree stump. It looked very comfortable.

"A short rest won't hurt," she thought. The mouse yawned and settled down for a quick nap.

Suddenly, the mouse heard a terrible roar. The stump shifted and shook. The mouse realized that she had not been sleeping on a stump at all—but on a lion's paw!

The lion lifted the mouse to his huge mouth and smacked his lips hungrily.

"Please don't hurt me!" cried the mouse. "I'd be such a tiny meal for you—only a small mouthful. My poor children will wonder where I am if I don't come home soon. Please spare me!"

The lion stared.

"You never know," the mouse added, "I might be able to help you one day."

To her surprise, the lion burst into laughter.

"How could a tiny mouse like you help a huge lion like me?"

Still laughing, the lion gently put the mouse on the ground.

"I can't see how you will ever be able to help me," he smiled, "but since you have made me laugh, you may go free."

The lion was still laughing as the mouse disappeared into the forest.

A few days later, the lion was roaming through the forest when all of a sudden . . .

WHOOSH!

. . . a hunter's net fell on top of him!

The lion twisted and struggled. He pulled and kicked. He scratched and tore. But no matter what he did, he could not get free. He was trapped.

The lion raised his head and roared with anger.

Far away, the little mouse was busy at her home at the edge of the forest. She heard the lion's angry roars.

Right away, she rushed to find him. She scampered over mossy rocks and tripped on fallen branches. She ran as fast as she could until she reached the spot where the lion lay.

Without stopping to think,
the little mouse climbed up onto
the lion's back. She began to
chew on the net's thick ropes.

The little mouse chewed
all night. At last, the net fell
apart. The lion crawled out.
He stretched his legs and shook
his mane with happiness. He
was free!

"Thank you, little one," said the lion gratefully. "You saved my life. But why did you bother to help me?"

The little mouse replied, "You were kind to me. Now I had the chance to be kind and help you. A good deed should always be returned."

AESOP

Aesop was a storyteller who lived more than 2,500 years ago. He lived so long ago, there isn't much information about him. Most people believe Aesop was a slave who lived in the area around the Mediterranean Sea—probably in or near the country of Greece.

Aesop's fables are known in almost every culture in the world, in almost every language. His fables are even *part* of some languages! Some common phrases come from Aesop's fables, such as "sour grapes" and "Don't count your chickens before they're hatched."

ABOUT FABLES

Fables are one of the oldest forms of stories. They are often short and funny, and have animals as the main characters. These animals act like people. Often, fables teach the reader a lesson. This is called a *moral*. A moral might teach right from wrong, or show how to act in good, kind ways. A moral might show what happens when someone makes a poor decision. Fables teach us how to live wisely.

ABOUT THE ILLUSTRATOR

Graham Percy was a famous illustrator of more than one hundred books. He was born and raised in New Zealand. He first studied art at the Elam School of Art in New Zealand and then moved to London, England, to study at the Royal College of Art.

Mr. Percy especially loved to draw animals, many types of which can be found in his books. He illustrated books on everything from mysteries to lullabies. He was even a designer for the animated film "Hugo the Hippo." Mr. Percy lived most of his life in London.